Lee Aucoin, *Creative Director*
Jamey Acosta, *Senior Editor*
Heidi Fiedler, *Editor*
Produced and designed by
Denise Ryan & Associates
Illustration © Clare Elsom
Rachelle Cracchiolo, *Publisher*

Teacher Created Materials
5301 Oceanus Drive
Huntington Beach, CA 92649-1030
http://www.tcmpub.com
Paperback: ISBN: 978-1-4333-5573-8
Library Binding: ISBN: 978-1-4807-1718-3

Soo Yun's Book

Written by Sharon Callen
Illustrated by Clare Elsom

Dear Soo Yun,

It has been wonderful having you at our school. We have learned many things about you and about your country, Korea.

We made this very special book all about you! We hope it helps you remember your friends in America. Maybe you will come and live in America again one day.

We will miss you.

Love from Class 2F

2

I remember meeting Soo Yun on the first day of school.

We didn't know each other, but I sat with her. She told me about her family. We both have a little brother and a big sister.

She is very funny and she likes to read a lot. Now she is my best friend, and I am sad she is leaving.

Mika

Soo Yun's little brother

Soo Yun

Soo Yun's big sister

My big sister

Me!

My little brother

5

I remember when I went to Soo Yun's house and we were given little dried fish. I didn't want to eat them, but Soo Yun told me they were her favorite snack. I tried one and it tasted great. I tried all kinds of different foods at her house. I miss sharing Soo Yun's little dried fish at school.

Annie

I remember when Soo Yun told us about where she lives in Korea. She lives in a city called Seoul. She showed us a map, a picture of a temple, and a photograph of her house.

Soo Yun told us she misses her grandpa and her cousins. She is going back to live in Seoul. We will miss her.

Joshua

9

I remember reading with Soo Yun. It was fun! We sat on the beanbags and read books together.

One day we were reading *Boris Keeps Fit*. We laughed when we saw Boris the dog doing push-ups. Soo Yun showed me some books from Korea. The writing is different, but Soo Yun can read it. I liked the pictures, but I couldn't read the words.

Alberto

1, 2, 3 하나, 둘, 셋

I remember when Soo Yun came to my birthday party. We went bowling. Soo Yun had never been bowling before, but she got a strike. She was very happy.

She gave me a toy cat from Seoul for my birthday. I keep it on the table by my bed. I will always remember Soo Yun, because I will think of her every time I look at my toy cat.

Claudia

13

I remember when Soo Yun sat next to me when we went on a field trip. We went over a long bridge and counted all the boats we could see.

Soo Yun told me her grandpa has a boat in Korea. He is a fisherman and he uses his boat to go fishing. Soo Yun has been fishing with her grandpa. She misses her grandpa.

Michael

Soo Yun and her Grandpa

I remember when it was Soo Yun's birthday. Soo Yun and her mom made little birthday cakes. There was a little cake for everyone in the class. The cakes tasted yummy! Soo Yun had a birthday party after school at her house. We were all invited and we had fun.

Sofia

17

I remember when I saw Soo Yun riding down our street. I talked to her and she told me all about her new bike. She got the bike for her birthday. It was a cool bike. She rides past my house almost every day. Sometimes, we go to the park together and ride our bikes.

Cruz

19

I remember when Soo Yun helped me because I didn't have my purple pencil at school. She let me use her purple pencil. Soo Yun is very kind.

I bought her some special pencils for her birthday. She brings them to school every day and lets me use them, too. I will miss her and I will write to her in Korea.

Nick

I remember when Soo Yun came to the park with me when it had just snowed. We made snow angels. We slid down the hill together on my toboggan. Soo Yun told me it sometimes snows in her country. Soo Yun loves the snow.

Helene

I remember when Soo Yun played the violin at the school concert. She was amazing. She has been learning the violin for four years. She started learning when she was three years old! She also plays the piano. Soo Yun might grow up to be a famous musician.

Jamie

I remember when Soo Yun won a special award for a book she made. She wrote about living in America and about all the friends she made. Soo Yun has lots of friends in America. She also has lots of friends in Korea. She is lucky because she has friends in two countries.

Amber

Goodbye and good luck, Soo Yun!

We will miss you very much.